ALISON OF ARABIA
by Nina Alexander

As members of the
MAGIC ATTIC CLUB,
we promise to
be best friends,
share all of our adventures in the attic,
use our imaginations,
have lots of fun together,
and remember—the real magic is in us.

Alison   Keisha

Heather   Megan

Contents

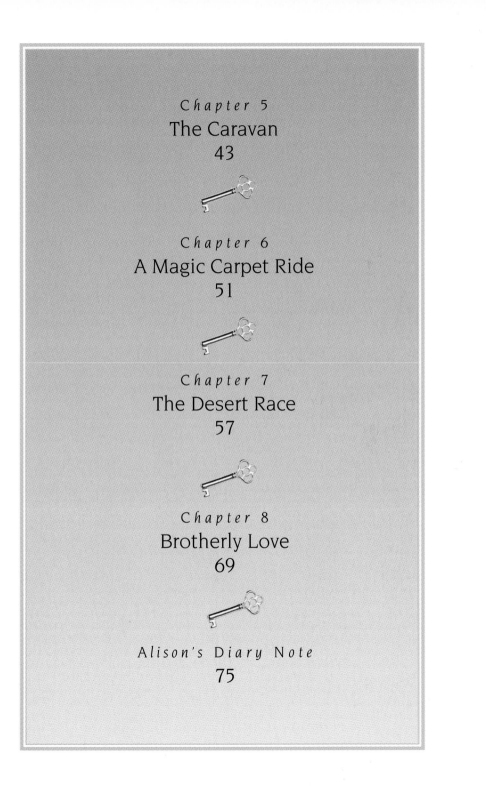

BAKING PLANS

ow about angel food cake?" Keisha Vance suggested. "Mmm, sounds yummy. But we have to make peanut butter cookies, too," Alison McCann rubbed her stomach hungrily. "They're my favorite."

It was a sunny Friday afternoon, and Keisha, Alison, and their other two best friends, Megan Ryder and Heather Hardin, were walking home from school. The four girls had volunteered to bring in baked goods on Monday for a school bake sale, and they were trying to decide what to make.

"I love angel food cake and peanut butter cookies," Heather said, tucking a strand of brown hair behind one ear. "But do you think we'll have time to make both?"

"Good point," Megan said. "Maybe we should just pick one recipe."

"I have a better idea," Alison said, swinging her book bag from one hand to the other. "Why don't we ask my mom to help us tomorrow? That way we can make all our favorites."

Heather nodded. "That's a great idea!"

"Come over to my house," Alison said. "We'll ask her right now."

The girls walked faster as they turned onto Primrose Lane. They passed their friend Ellie Goodwin's rambling white Victorian house. Together the four girls had discovered that Ellie's attic held a wonderful secret. Whenever any of them tried on one of the outfits she found up there and looked in the mirror, she was carried away to another time and place. After their first adventure, the four friends had formed the Magic Attic Club. But today the girls were so excited about their errand that they hurried up the McCanns' driveway without a thought for Ellie or her marvelous attic.

As soon as they entered Alison's house, the girls headed for the kitchen. It was in its usual state of chaos. Two saucepans bubbled away on the stove, and half a batch of fancy cookies was laid out on a baking sheet. The other half of the cookie dough was on the counter waiting to be rolled out and shaped. Mrs. McCann was slicing bread while Alison's older brother, Mark, sat at the table reading a sports magazine. The spicy scent of tomato sauce flavored the air.

"Hi, Mom," Alison said. "We have a favor to ask."

Mrs. McCann glanced up. "Hi, Alison. Hi, girls," she said, sounding tired. "You can ask, but I'm not making any promises."

Alison didn't pay any attention to the comment. With two parents with demanding jobs and three brothers, Alison knew enough to speak up when she wanted something. "We were planning to bake all day tomorrow for the bake sale at school. Will you help us?"

Mrs. McCann sighed. "I'm sorry, sweetie," she said. "Tomorrow is definitely out. Mark has a baseball game in the morning, and your father and I promised we'd go watch. After that, I'll be busy getting ready for the cocktail party I'm catering in the evening."

That definitely wasn't the answer Alison had been expecting. "But Mom," she protested, "you've got to help us! We can't do all that baking by ourselves."

"True." Mark looked up from his magazine with a grin. "Who knows how many people this bunch could poison if they got the chance."

Mrs. McCann shook her head. "I'm sorry, Alison. Tomorrow is out of the question," she said firmly.

"Can't you let Dad go to the stupid game by himself?" Alison asked.

Mark glared at her. "It's not stupid," he retorted hotly. "We're playing Oakview tomorrow. And I want Mom and Dad to come. You can have your cookie-making party some other time."

"We'll be there, honey," Mrs. McCann told Mark. Then she turned to Alison with a slight frown. "And for the last time, I'm sorry, but I just can't help you tomorrow."

Megan spoke up politely before Alison could protest further. "That's okay, Mrs. McCann. We understand. Do you have any free time on Sunday? Maybe we could do some baking then if you're not too tired."

"I suppose that would be okay," Mrs. McCann said. "What were you thinking of making?" When the girls told her their ideas, she nodded. "All right. I'll pick up the ingredients while I'm out tomorrow and we'll spend

Sunday afternoon baking. How does that sound?"

"Great," chorused Megan, Keisha, and Heather.

But Alison just shrugged. "I guess it'll do."

"Of course it will," Heather said quickly, giving Alison a worried look. "That way our cookies will be fresher on Monday anyway."

"Good," Mrs. McCann said. "Now that that's settled, Alison, could you set the table? Dinner will be ready soon."

"Isn't it Mark's turn?" Alison glanced at her brother.

"Nice try, sis," Mark replied. "It's your turn."

"It seems like it's always my turn," Alison muttered.

"Don't worry, Ali," Heather said. "We'll help." Alison went to the drawer to get the silverware while Megan and Keisha took plates and glasses out of the cabinets.

"Hey, I just thought of something," Heather said as she set out place mats. "Since we're not baking until Sunday, we can go try the new in-line skating course. It opens tomorrow, remember?"

The bicycle paths at the park had become so crowded

with in-line skaters that the park manager had decided to build a separate set of trails just for them.

"I almost forgot about that," Keisha said. "All the kids at school are going to be there. We have to go!"

The thought of trying the new course immediately made Alison feel much better. In fact, she realized, it was downright lucky her mother was busy the next day, or the girls would have missed the exciting opening day. "Definitely," she agreed.

Mr. McCann arrived home from work just as the girls finished setting the table. "Hi, Dad," Alison greeted him cheerfully. "Guess what? Mom's going to help us bake on Sunday, so we'll be sure to have the best stuff at the bake sale on Monday."

"That's great, honey," her father said. He said hello to Alison's friends, then kissed his wife and tousled Mark's hair. "By the way, Alison, it looks like your mother and I will need your help tomorrow. One of my real estate clients called today and invited me to play golf after Mark's baseball game. Since your mother has errands to run after the game, the boys will have to stay home this time. And we'll need you to baby-sit."

Alison's jaw dropped. "Tomorrow? But we're going skating tomorrow," she said. "Why can't Mark baby-sit?"

"I have the game, remember?" Mark said, hardly

glancing up from his magazine. "And the coach promised to take us out for pizza afterward."

"But we already made plans," Alison protested, giving her friends a desperate glance. "Can't you play golf some other day, Dad?"

Mr. McCann sighed. "Believe me, I wish I could. I was looking forward to a quiet day at home tomorrow. But this is one of my most important clients. I can't turn him down if I want to make this sale."

Alison turned to her mother. "Can't you take the twins with you?"

Her mother frowned. "Alison, I have a lot to do tomorrow," she said. "I'm sorry, but this isn't up for discussion. You'll have to go to the park with your friends another time. Tomorrow, you're baby-sitting."

"We'd better get going," said Megan.

Alison walked her friends to the door. "I can't believe this," she moaned.

"Don't worry, Ali," Keisha comforted her. "At least your mom agreed to help us with the cookies."

"Not on the day we wanted her to, though," Alison pointed out. "Thanks to Mark's stupid game." She shook her head, looking determined. "Anyway, there's no way I'm going to waste a perfectly good Saturday afternoon here when I could be skating with you guys.

I'll figure something out. Don't worry."

"We'll stop by on our way to the park tomorrow," Heather promised. But she didn't look very hopeful.

Chapter TWO

BABY-SITTING
BLUES

he next morning at breakfast, Alison toyed with her cereal while Mr. McCann drank coffee and Mrs. McCann made a list of her errands. Mark, wearing his baseball uniform, shoveled cereal into his mouth. The twins had finished eating and were coloring in the next room.

"Hey Mark," Alison said. "What time is your pizza party over?"

Mark looked up, milk dripping down his chin. "I

don't know," he said. "Why?"

Alison gave him her most winning smile. "I was just wondering if you'd come home and take over for me when you're finished."

"Alison," Mrs. McCann said before Mark could answer, "we don't ask for your help that often. We expect you to stay here and look after the twins until your father or I get home—not Mark." She returned to her list, and Mark smirked at his sister.

Mr. McCann glanced at Alison over the top of his newspaper. "Don't worry, honey," he said. "I'll try to get home as early as I can to take over, okay?"

"Okay," Alison said glumly. Her father's golf games usually went on all day. "What about you, Mom? What time do you think you'll be home?"

Mrs. McCann didn't even look up from her list. It was already two pages long. "I doubt I'll make it back here before the party," she said. "I have to be at the country club by four o'clock to set up. I'll probably head straight there when I finish my errands."

"I'm ready to go when you are," Mark told his parents, standing up and setting his bowl in the sink.

Mr. McCann fished his car keys out of his pocket. "I'll go start the car."

"Don't forget, Alison, Ellie Goodwin is right next door

if you need anything." Mrs. McCann tucked her list into her purse. "And the emergency numbers are on the refrigerator." She called good-bye to the twins and disappeared through the garage door.

Mark grinned at Alison as he followed their parents out of the house. "Have fun today, sis. I'll think of you when I head over to check out the new skating course."

Alison clenched her fists. It was bad enough that Mark had to ruin her fun. Did he have to rub it in, too?

Megan, Keisha, and Heather stopped by Alison's house right after lunch, carrying their skates. Alison led them into the living room, dodging the foam football that the twins were tossing back and forth.

"Thank goodness you're here," she said. "I haven't had anyone human to talk to all day."

Megan laughed as Steven and Jason tried to retrieve the football from the fish tank. "Oh, come on, Ali," she said. "You have to admit the twins are awfully cute."

"Spoken like an only child," Keisha said.

Alison nodded. "I wish I were an only child," she said,

leaping forward just in time to stop the tank from tipping over. She plunged her hand into the water, startling the fish, and came up with the dripping football.

"Here." She handed it to Steven. "Go wipe it off before you throw it again." The twins ran off toward the bathroom, and Alison sighed with relief.

"Bad day, huh?" Heather asked.

Alison collapsed on the couch next to Keisha. "It could be worse," she admitted. "The twins aren't so bad. It's Mark who's a big jerk. And my parents don't even realize it. He has them all fooled. Does anyone want to trade families with me? I'll be glad to pay you."

Megan laughed. "Come on, Ali," she said. "Your family is great."

"That's easy for you to say," Alison said. "You don't have to arrange your life around a bunch of brothers."

"Brothers and sisters can be a pain sometimes," Keisha admitted. "Still, you have to admit they do make life more interesting."

"Maybe yours do," Alison said. "But would you want to switch with me?" She turned to Heather, who was perched on a chair near the couch. "What about you, Heather?" she said. "I'd love to have an older sister instead of an older brother for a change. Even yours."

Heather grinned, then glanced at her watch. "I guess we'd better get going," she said. "We don't want to miss the opening ceremony. Sorry, Ali."

"Don't worry about it," Alison said glumly. She walked her friends to the door. "By the way, if you happen to see Mark there, try to run over his toe or something, okay?"

Keisha just smiled. "We'll call you tonight," she promised.

"And we'll go with you soon so you can try the new course for yourself," Megan said. "Maybe we'll have time tomorrow afternoon."

Two hours later, Alison was in the kitchen pouring the twins glasses of juice when she heard the front door opening. It's probably Mark popping in to tell me about all the fun I'm missing, she thought in annoyance. This was all Mark's fault. If he weren't around, she would be the oldest, and maybe she would be the one who got all the attention and was allowed to do whatever she liked.

But it wasn't Mark—it was Alison's father. "Hi, kids," he said with a smile, walking into the kitchen. "My game ended earlier than I thought. So you're off the hook, Alison."

"Great," Alison muttered.

Her father looked surprised. "Don't you want to go to the park and catch up with your friends?"

"It's too late," Alison said. "I'll never be able to find them."

Chapter
Three

MEETING A GENIE

ventually, Alison got tired of moping around the house. She decided to go look for her friends after all. "I'm going to the park," she yelled to her father, who was upstairs with the twins. She grabbed her skates and hurried out the door.

As she passed Ellie's house, Alison had a great idea. She would see if Ellie wanted her to take her terrier, Monty, to the park for a run. "That way I'll have company even if I don't find the others," she murmured to herself as she reached Ellie's shady front porch and rang the bell.

"Hello, Alison," Ellie greeted her, letting her into the wide entry hall. "What a surprise. I thought you were baby-sitting today. I hope nothing's wrong."

Alison shook her head and bent down to pet Monty, who came racing up to greet her. "My dad just got home," she said. "Thank goodness. I was afraid I was going to be stuck baby-sitting the twins for the rest of my life. It's all Mark's fault. He drives me crazy."

The corners of Ellie's bright blue eyes crinkled when she smiled. "Sometimes brothers do that," she said. "What happened?"

Alison told Ellie the whole story. As she talked, she felt angrier and angrier. "My parents do everything Mark wants them to. He's always messing up my life one way or another."

"Oh, come now, Alison," Ellie said. "I know—" She was interrupted by the ringing of the doorbell. "Oh, dear. That's my next pupil, for her piano lesson." She touched Alison on the shoulder. "Why don't you go up to the attic for awhile? If you're still feeling bad later, we can talk more after the lesson is over."

Before long Alison was in Ellie's large, cedar-scented attic. Every time she went there, she found different treasures and fascinating objects. This time she decided to dig down to the very bottom of the large trunk near the windows. She swung open the heavy lid and plunged her arms into layers of fabric. Her hands touched silk, satin, wool, and taffeta. But she continued digging until she felt the bottom of the trunk and a whisper-thin bit of fabric. As she started to pull it out, her hand hit something cool and hard.

"I wonder what that is," she said to herself. Curious, she removed the other things from the trunk, piling them neatly on the colorfully patterned oriental rug. Soon she uncovered a small, gracefully shaped lamp made of shiny brass. It was wrapped in the folds of the silky outfit she had felt. "Interesting," she murmured, examining the lamp's exotic, curved shape.

Then Alison turned her attention to the outfit itself. She held up a pair of rose-pink silk harem pants with a shimmering waistband. There was also a matching top and vest, decorated with beads and embroidery, a pair of gold slippers, and a headpiece with a sheer veil attached.

At the very bottom of the trunk were several bracelets.

"Wow," Alison said out loud. "It's like something out of the Arabian Nights."

Before long Alison had changed into the gossamer clothing. One of the bracelets was too large for her wrist, so she put it around her ankle, where it fit perfectly. She liked the soft, tinkling sound it made when she walked.

She picked up the brass lamp and tucked it under her arm. Then she walked over to the gilt-framed mirror.

"Wow," she said with a grin as she twirled before the mirror, watching as the reflection of the soft silken folds of her pants began to shimmer. "My friends wouldn't believe their eyes if they saw me now!"

Suddenly Alison found herself staring at her reflection in the shiny surface of a huge, polished brass tray. She looked around at a large, high-ceilinged room. Vividly colored rugs carpeted the floor. Brass, copper, and silver gleamed from every corner, and elaborate frescoes decorated the walls. The few pieces of furniture included a long, low bench piled high with fancy tasseled cushions of silk and velvet and a table intricately inlaid with gold and jewels. "Amazing," Alison whispered. "Where am I?"

One wall was lined with large windows shaped like upside-down teardrops. Squinting against the bright, hot sunlight pouring through, Alison hurried over to look out.

The window overlooked a sumptuous courtyard garden surrounded by narrow city streets teeming with people. But the city didn't look like any that Alison had ever seen. The buildings were squat and square, with few windows. Instead of brick or stone, they were made out of some kind of material the color of desert sand. All the men she saw wore turbans and long, flowing garments, and the women were so covered by robes and veils that only their eyes showed. There were no cars or bicycles. The few people who weren't on foot rode tall, shambling camels or horses with flowing manes and tails. Goats and sheep and children wandered about here and there.

I've got to get out there and see this, Alison thought, and she hurried toward a wide archway. It led into another room, smaller than the first but just as opulent. This one appeared to be a bedroom, but before Alison could look around, a pretty, exotic-looking girl stepped into view.

"Greetings, Princess Almira," said the girl with a slight bow. "Allow me to introduce myself. I am Fatima. I will be at your command during your visit to your uncle." Fatima was dressed in the same style as Alison, though her clothes were plainer and she wore no jewelry. She had large, dark eyes and appeared to be about Alison's own age.

"Um, greetings, Fatima," Alison said. She absent-mindedly tossed the brass lamp from hand to hand. "Just call me Ali, okay?"

Fatima's eyes widened. "Oh, forgive my protest, Princess, for I am yours to command in all things," she cried. "But how could I, a mere maidservant, refer to the sultan's niece in this manner? Please, I beg most humbly, do not ask this of me!"

The girl looked so upset that Alison felt sorry for her. "Okay, okay," she said hastily. "Forget I mentioned it."

Fatima gave her a grateful smile. "It is already forgotten, Princess."

"Good," Alison said. So I'm the sultan's niece, she thought. This could be interesting. She headed toward the archway to the sitting room, but her shoe caught on the edge of one of the rugs. She almost tripped but caught herself just in time. The lamp flew out of her hand and fell to the floor.

As she bent to pick it up, Alison really thought about the lamp for the first time. "Hmm," she said. "I wonder…" She tentatively rubbed the side of the lamp.

Suddenly there was a blinding flash of silver light, and a tall, silvery-pale man in golden robes materialized before her. He had a thin face with enormous eyes the color of the night sky. On his head was a large white-and-gold satin turban with a huge jewel winking in the middle of it. The jewel seemed to glow with a light from within, and Alison found herself almost mesmerized by its brightness.

"Good day, Princess," the odd-looking stranger said in a deep, musical voice. "I am the genie of the lamp, and you are now my master. I am here to grant you any three wishes your heart desires. Your wish is my command."

Chapter Four

THREE WISHES

 lison could hardly believe her eyes and ears. Was it true? Was she face to face with a real genie?

"I can really have any three things I want?" she exclaimed. "Wow! Thanks, genie!"

"My name is Maimun," said the genie.

Alison liked the name. It sounded like "my moon."

"And there is no need to thank me," Maimun went on. "As a genie, I do as my masters wish, with no need or desire for gratitude."

"Oh, sorry," Alison said. Obviously Maimun took his job very seriously. "I didn't realize that. I've never met a genie before."

"There is no need to apologize, master," Maimun replied.

Alison swallowed back a giggle. The genie looked so dignified that she didn't think it would be proper to laugh. "So how many masters have you had before me?" she asked curiously.

The genie seemed surprised by the question. "That I cannot say."

"Is that some kind of genie rule or something?" Alison asked.

Maimun shook his head. "No," he said in his booming, musical voice. "I just never kept count."

Just then Fatima entered. Alison waited for her to say something about Maimun, but the maidservant only bowed.

"I will go now to fetch your midday meal, Princess, unless you require anything else of me," she said.

"No, that's all right," Alison said. This was getting better all the time. Not only did she have a genie at her command, but she had servants begging to wait on her. Being a princess was great. "Thank you, Fatima." After the girl had left, Alison turned to Maimun. "She didn't even notice you," she commented.

"I am invisible to all but my master," the genie replied.

"Oh." Alison paused, trying to decide what to wish for. In fairy tales, people usually wished for gold and jewels, but Alison really wasn't interested in stuff like that. Besides, if she was a princess, she probably didn't need it anyway. She tried to think of something more exciting, but nothing good came to mind.

"I just can't decide," she said at last. "Do you have any ideas, Maimun?"

Maimun's serious expression didn't change. "My only idea is to serve my master."

That wasn't much help. But suddenly Alison had an idea of her own.

"I know," she said. "Maybe I should ask for a horse. I've always wanted my own horse."

"Is that your wish?" the genie asked. "All you must do is begin your sentence with 'I wish,' and it shall be done."

Before Alison could answer Fatima re-entered, balancing two trays piled high with food. She set them down on a table near Alison, almost walking into Maimun as she did so. Alison nearly laughed out loud as the genie darted out of the maidservant's path.

Alison peered closely at one silver plate, which held what looked like gigantic raisins. "What are these?"

she asked curiously.

Fatima looked a little surprised. "Sugared dates—your royal favorite, according to the servants in your own palace. Is that not correct?"

"Oh. Of course, how foolish of me," Alison said quickly. "Thanks." Fatima bowed and quietly glided out of the room.

Alison picked up one of the dates and bit into it. It was delicious—sticky and sweet and a bit chewy. She had never tasted anything quite so flavorful. She spit out the hard pit and eagerly reached for another date, and then another. Before long, she had eaten the whole trayful.

"Mmm, I wish I had about a million more of these," Alison murmured, licking her fingers as she finished the last one.

Maimun, with a very strange expression on his face, suddenly made an elaborate gesture with his hands— too fast for Alison to follow. Before she could ask what he was doing, Fatima rushed back into the bedroom. "Princess!" she cried, with a distressed frown. "Something most strange has happened in the sitting room."

Alison went to the archway. She looked out and her

jaw dropped. The sitting room was stuffed from floor to ceiling with plump, juicy sugared dates. "Don't tell me..." she said.

Maimun crossed his arms and surveyed the dates. "A wish is a wish," he said. "I did tell you the rules."

"Don't worry, Fatima," Alison told the servant girl, thinking fast. Fatima was still looking around in shock. "I asked for these." Maybe she hadn't meant to make the wish, but at least now she knew that Maimun was for real. She would just have to be more careful from now on.

She reached forward, grabbed a handful of dates, and stuffed them in her mouth. They tasted just as good as the first batch, and she ate greedily until she could eat no more, letting the pits fall on the floor. "Yum," she murmured at last, staggering back into the bedroom and sinking onto the cushions.

It didn't take long for Alison to regret her actions. For one thing, she was trapped in her room by the leftover dates. She and Fatima had to shout for help, then wait while a whole army of servants came to clear away the mess. Then her stomach began churning, and soon she felt so sick she could hardly stand up.

She glanced at the genie with a groan. "Ugh, remind me never to eat that much again."

"Never eat that much again, Princess," Maimun

repeated obediently. Alison wondered for a moment if he was making fun of her. But right now she felt so miserable that she didn't really care. She was dying to explore this fascinating land and to use her two remaining wishes, but she couldn't keep her eyes open.

"I feel almost bad enough to wish this stomachache away," Alison said, flopping down on the soft bed. "But not quite," she added hurriedly. "That wasn't a real wish. I'll have to get back to you on those, okay, Maimun?"

"There is no need to ask my leave, master," the genie replied. With another flash of brilliant silver light, he disappeared.

The next morning Alison's stomach felt much better. She grabbed the lamp and headed out to explore. Each room held new and more amazing wonders, from exotic birds in golden cages to room-sized frescoes depicting fantastic scenes to gigantic statues encrusted with jewels. And everywhere Alison went, servants actually begged to serve her!

"Most Exalted Princess," cried one young man, stepping in front of her and bowing all the way to the floor. "You mustn't tire your tender feet by walking down this lengthy hallway. Please allow me to carry you to your destination."

Alison waved him away. "There's no need for that," she protested. "I can walk." But before she had gone a dozen steps, another servant approached.

"Princess," he exclaimed. "My humblest apologies for not realizing sooner that you were near. May I provide you some service?"

Once again, Alison shook her head. "I'm just looking around," she said firmly. "I don't need anything." The servant seemed unconvinced but stepped aside to let her pass.

Alison shook her head and walked on. She peeked through the next door she came to. Inside, dozens of servants bustled around a large room, preparing trays of tempting foods. She guessed that she had just found the royal kitchen. "Your Royal Highness," one of the cooks cried when she saw her. "To what do we owe the great honor of your visit?"

"Oh, nothing," Alison said. "I'm just exploring."

Another cook stepped forward, holding a silver tray out. "Would you care for a small snack?" he offered. "We have just prepared this plate of sugared dates."

Alison shuddered, feeling her stomach churn. "No, that's okay," she said quickly. "Thanks anyway." Suddenly she had an idea. "Have you seen my uncle lately?" she asked. "I thought I'd see what he's doing."

The cook set the platter down immediately. "No need to weary yourself in locating the sultan, Princess," he exclaimed. "Please allow me to take a message to your uncle while you return to your chambers and rest your delicate feet."

Alison glanced down at her feet. They did look more delicate than usual in the soft slippers, but they felt just as strong and agile as always. And the last thing they— or any other part of her—wanted to do was go back and lie around in her bedchamber. "Never mind," she said. "I'm sure I'll find him. Forget I asked."

The cook bowed low. "As you wish," he said humbly.

Alison couldn't even take a step without someone running up and offering to take it for her. She hurried out of the kitchen and down the hall, ducking behind a pillar as another servant came around the corner. She waited until the woman had hurried past, then continued on her way.

At least there was one person Alison could talk to. Well, maybe not a person exactly. Maimun might be a

little weird, but he was the closest thing she had to a
friend here. Checking to make sure the hall was empty,
she pulled out the lamp and rubbed it. The genie
appeared instantly. "Yes, master?" he said. "Have you
decided on your second wish?"

"Not yet," Alison said. "I was wondering if you knew
where the sultan is."

"Come, I will show you." Maimun led the way through
a maze of passageways to an arched doorway draped with
thick, heavy fabric. Beyond, Alison caught a glimpse of a

cavernous room with a cluster of people at the far end.

Maimun moved the curtain aside a little. "This is the throne room."

Now Alison saw that the people were gathered around a huge throne of gleaming wood carved in the shape of a gigantic peacock. The peacock's beak was fashioned out of gold, and its body and feathers were decorated with jewels of every possible color, shape, and size.

Alison let out a low whistle. "Pretty fancy seat," she commented. "Let me guess—that must be the sultan."

The man on the throne was large and stern-looking, with weathered brown skin and a turban almost as elaborate as Maimun's.

"That is the sultan," the genie said, "the supreme ruler of this kingdom. Perhaps you might wait awhile if you desire to speak with him. At the moment he and his advisers are discussing the caravans that have arrived or departed this week. He may not wish to be disturbed."

"Caravans?" Alison said, suddenly interested. "What caravans?"

Maimun let the curtain drop over the archway again, then turned to gaze at Alison with his dark, fathomless eyes. "This is a desert kingdom, Princess," he said. "A camel caravan is the best means of transportation for people and supplies."

"Can I go on a caravan?" Alison asked. Riding a camel sounded like fun.

"You can do anything you like. You have only to wish it so," Maimun reminded her.

Alison shrugged. "I don't want to waste a wish if I don't have to," she said. "I'm a princess, right? I should be able to go on a caravan if I want."

The genie looked grave. "Perhaps your uncle is more lenient than most men," he said. "But I have not known of many young ladies your age who were allowed to experience the rigors of the desert unless absolutely necessary."

"You're kidding, right?" Alison stared at Maimun. "Are you telling me I can't go on a caravan because I'm a girl?" She couldn't believe it. Having the servants treat her like she couldn't do a thing for herself had been one thing. But this was a completely different matter.

"I am sorry, master," Maimun said. "I do not usually

comment on my masters' affairs, but for my part I see no reason why you are not as capable of riding in a caravan as any boy."

"Thanks, Maimun," Alison said gratefully. The genie's words made her feel a little bit better.

Maimun nodded slightly. "Of course," he went on, "my opinion means nothing. It is your uncle who must give his permission, and it is unlikely he will do so."

Alison peeked between the heavy curtains again at the figure on the throne across the vast room. From this distance the mens' voices were no more than a low murmur. "I wish there were some way I could go on that caravan without the sultan knowing about it," she muttered, thinking out loud. "I'd do anything!"

Maimun's hands began moving immediately, tracing the lightning-fast pattern Alison had seen before. "Your wish is my command, Princess," the genie said. "There is a way. You will go on the caravan—disguised as a boy."

Chapter
Five

THE
CARAVAN

efore Alison realized what was happening, she
found herself nestled in an elaborately
embroidered saddle high atop the steep, swaying back of
a camel. She lifted her hand to her head. Her hair was
tucked out of sight under a turban. She felt the weight of
the magic lamp in a pocket of her robe.

"Wow," she whispered. "I guess I've got to be careful
with this wishing stuff."

"That is correct," said Maimun, who was floating

beside her. "You made a wish; I granted it. That is my purpose."

"But it was an accident," Alison said. "Can't you take it back?"

"What's done is done," the genie said solemnly. "The others will know you as Ahmad." With that he disappeared.

"Come back!" Alison whispered desperately. "Maimun? Where are you?"

The boy on the camel ahead of her turned around. "Hey, Ahmad," he called. "Who are you talking to?"

"He's having a conversation with his camel," shouted the boy behind Alison. "I wonder if the camel talked back." Both boys laughed, and Alison felt her face turning red. She would have to be careful about talking to Maimun when other people were around.

She settled back, doing her best to get comfortable on the lumpy saddle and adjust to the camel's swaying, shambling stride. Maybe she hadn't meant to make this wish, but that didn't mean she couldn't enjoy herself.

Alison looked around. There were about thirty camels, and they had just left the outskirts of the city. Ahead stretched a seemingly endless expanse of desert. The sunlight reflecting off the bleached sand was so bright that she had to squint. After a moment, she noticed a strong and decidedly unpleasant odor rising from her camel, "Ugh," she said. "You stink." But

the camel paid no attention to the insult, and soon Alison was distracted by another discomfort. It was hot—really hot. The sun beat down relentlessly, and she had started to sweat. She did her best to ignore the heat and enjoy the ride. But after an hour, with nothing but dune after dune of sand to look at, she was sweaty, she was uncomfortable, and she was getting really thirsty.

If I wish for rain, she thought, it will probably be one of those huge, sudden floods like I saw in that documentary about deserts.

Alison sighed and squinted at the desert stretching away in all directions. Where were they going? When would they get there? If she didn't get something to drink soon, she didn't know what she would do. She pictured a tall, icy glass of lemonade, dripping with beads of condensation. The image was so inviting that her mouth dropped open, and she could almost taste the sweet, tart liquid in her mouth.

Suddenly she felt something else in her mouth. "Blech!" she cried, spitting quickly. A very annoyed fly buzzed away, and Alison quickly wiped her tongue with her hand. Then she shut her mouth firmly and kept it that way.

She was relieved when a cry of "Oasis!" rose from the front of the caravan. Finally, she thought, leaning forward

to get a look at the lush stand
of palm trees just ahead.
Maybe now she
would get something
to drink. When the
caravan reached
the edge of the
oasis, the man in
the lead blew a
loud, shrill note
on a wooden flute to
bring them to a halt and order the camels to kneel.

Alison waited impatiently for her camel to settle to
the ground, then slid off with relief. "Whew," she said,
rubbing her aching backside.

The camel ignored her, so she hurried off to find some
water. After she had drunk her fill from the clear, cool
spring bubbling up in the shade of the trees, she sat
down on the grass to rest.

Before long, several other boys from the caravan had
gathered nearby to talk—bragging was more like it. One
of them gave the others a superior glance. "This caravan
is fine, but if I wanted to, I could be at our destination
already," he said. "Don't forget, my grandfather owns a
real magic carpet that can take me anywhere I want to go

at the speed of the fastest sandstorm."

"It takes no skill to ride a magic carpet, Faisal," scoffed a boy they had called Jakeem. "I would much rather ride my horse, Borak. Soon I'll show the entire kingdom that I'm the best rider of them all, and that Borak is the finest steed in the land."

"If that's true, why aren't you riding in the race today?" challenged another.

A race? Alison listened more carefully. This could be the most interesting news she'd heard all day.

"My father insists that my horse requires more training before he is ready to compete," Jakeem admitted, looking a little embarrassed. "But he promised that next year I may ride. And I promised that I'll win!"

Another boy started bragging about being the fastest runner in the kingdom, but Alison had stopped listening. She had to find out more about the race. It sounded like a lot more fun than this ride had turned out to be.

Alison tiptoed away from the group and found a secluded spot behind a stand of trees. She took out the lamp and summoned Maimun.

"Yes, master?" he said, appearing immediately. "How are you enjoying the caravan?"

Alison grimaced. "It's not exactly what I was expecting," she said. "Listen, I have a question. Do you know anything about a race today?"

"The desert race," Maimun said. "The best horses and young riders in the land will be competing before a large crowd, including the sultan himself. As you know, Arabian horses are renowned for their stamina, and the race will follow a lengthy and difficult course through the desert."

That sounded exciting to Alison. "When does it start?"

"In exactly one hour."

Alison's heart dropped. She had already been with the caravan for more than twice that long. She would never make it back in time on her camel even if she started right now. But she knew there was another way if she wanted to use it…

"Come on, Ahmad, we're getting ready to leave," one of the boys called.

It took Alison a second to realize he was talking to her, but then she stuck the lamp back in her pocket and rejoined the others. Maimun had disappeared, and she wasn't sure whether to call him back or not. Did she want to use her final wish to go back to the palace for the race? It didn't seem like much of a wish, but Alison had had enough of this one. The thought of riding on was almost unbearable.

As she pondered her options, she walked to her camel and picked up its lead rope. The beast obviously wasn't in the mood for any more walking, either. It resisted her attempts to lead it away from the shade. And when she yanked at the rope in annoyance, it looked down at her—and spit right in her face.

"Ugh!" Alison cried, dropping the rope and lifting the edge of her robe to wipe away the camel spit. "This stinks. I wish I were somewhere else!"

Chapter Six

A MAGIC CARPET RIDE

Just in the nick of time, Alison realized her error.

As Maimun materialized in a flash of silver, Alison thought fast. "Um, somewhere else—namely, back at the palace getting ready to ride the fastest horse in the land in the race," she added hastily. She remembered Faisal's bragging and decided to go all out. "And I want to be taken there on a magic carpet. Oh, and I want to look like a girl again, of course."

Maimun looked a little taken aback at the lengthy

wish, but he didn't protest. "Your desire is my command," he said. "Let us depart." With a wave of his hands, a flying carpet appeared before them. It was woven of multi-colored threads, and tassels hung from each corner.

Alison pushed the pink veil away from her face and climbed aboard. Sitting on the flying carpet felt sort of like floating on a rubber raft, except softer and drier. And unlike a raft, the carpet seemed to vibrate gently with its own energy. "Coming, Maimun?" She patted the carpet invitingly. "Oh! Unless you have to go now that I made my last wish."

The genie shook his head. "My duty is to stay until your final wish has run its course." He floated over and settled down beside her.

The carpet climbed quickly into the sky, and for a second Alison's stomach flip-flopped. While it floated for a moment above the oasis, Alison saw several men tugging at her camel's lead rope. It had knelt down again and refused to move. When she saw that, she wasn't at all sorry about using her final wish to escape. Still, she had almost made another big mistake—who knew how Maimun would have interpreted "somewhere else."

Alison sat back to enjoy the ride. It was a lot more comfortable than the caravan had been. A cool breeze ruffled her hair and lifted her veil as the carpet zoomed across the desert. They were moving too fast to see much, but Alison had seen enough sand dunes already, and it felt great to be moving so fast. She tossed her head, happy to have her long hair free of the heavy turban. Within minutes the city came into sight on the horizon.

"This is great, Maimun," Alison cried. "Can we take a look around?" Her stomach lurched as they swooped suddenly downward, almost grazing the prayer tower of a mosque.

A second later she and Maimun were hovering just above an area packed with open-air stalls. Merchants called to the shoppers, cajoling them to purchase everything imaginable, from nuts and fruits to brass and silver jewelry to trinkets and objects Alison couldn't even recognize.

"This bazaar is the main marketplace for the entire city," Maimun said. "One can buy nearly anything here."

Alison heard one merchant arguing heatedly with a customer. "What's going on there?" Alison asked, a little

worried that a fight would break out.

"Do not be alarmed," Maimun replied. "They are only haggling over the price. It is customary—the merchants expect it."

"Oh."

The magic carpet banked and rose, making Alison's stomach flip-flop again. "And now," the genie said, "we must get back. The racers will be lining up soon."

"I can't wait," Alison exclaimed. "Let's go!"

Chapter

Seven

THE DESERT RACE

he carpet deposited Alison and Maimun in the
royal stable yard. A horse
was standing a few feet away,
fully saddled and stomping
his feet impatiently. Alison
gasped when she saw
him. "He's gorgeous!"
she exclaimed.
"That is Shihab,"

the genie said. "He will be your mount for the race."

Alison took a step forward. Shihab was a tall stallion, and his neck arched gracefully to an elegant head. The horse snorted when he saw Alison and pointed his velvety nose down to sniff her outstretched hand.

"You like him," Maimun said. It wasn't really a question, but Alison nodded.

"I love him," she declared. "I can't believe I really get to ride him."

"Come," the genie said. "You must hurry or you will miss the start of the race." He watched as Alison led the stallion to a large boulder and used it to mount. The horse stood calmly until she was settled in the saddle, then pranced to one side. She had to grab his long, silky mane to keep her balance.

Alison laughed. "He's awfully spirited," she said approvingly. "I bet that means he's fast, too, right?"

The genie didn't reply to the question. He was gazing at Alison with a thoughtful expression in his huge eyes. "Perhaps it is not my place to say so," he said. "But your uncle will certainly not approve of your choice to race. You have wished it, and it will happen. But it is your decision whether to cause the sultan anger and concern during the race by riding undisguised."

Alison's temper began to flare—once again, she

wasn't supposed to do something she wanted. At the same time, she understood that Maimun didn't want her to upset the sultan unnecessarily, and she made herself stay calm.

"Maybe you have a point." She sighed. "I guess I could disguise myself as a boy again."

When Alison, Maimun, and Shihab arrived at the edge of the desert, the racers were lining up at the starting line. It was a beautiful sight. Spirited Arabian horses of every color snorted and pawed at the earth. Boys from seven to seventeen were mounted on them. Throngs of people cheered from all sides, and Alison recognized the sultan standing on a dais at the far end of the starting line. She tugged her turban a little lower over her forehead and lifted the edge of her tunic to tighten the rope belt on her pants. After taking her place in line, she reached forward to pat Shihab on the neck. "Ready, boy?" She glanced to either side. On her right, a skittish dapple-gray mare did her best to unseat her rider, a lithe teenage boy. To the left, a younger boy sat calmly astride a mahogany-bay stallion.

Alison turned back to the rolling dunes ahead of her. In the distance, she saw the rocky foothills of the mountains that stretched away north of the city. Maimun

had already explained the route to her. It would be a true test of the graceful desert horses' endurance as well as their speed. They would run toward the mountains,
then turn to
circle a large
outcropping a few

hundred yards to the east. Then they would trace a path around and over the nearest foothills before returning for the finish.

"Do not worry," the genie had told her. "There is no need for you to remember every step of the route. Your horse knows the way. And men are posted to mark the course."

Alison had felt very relieved at that. "Good," she said. "I'd hate to gallop off and get lost somewhere in the desert."

It seemed to take forever before everyone was lined up and ready. Alison did her best to stay calm, though, knowing that her horse could sense her mood. She could tell that he was raring to go, and she didn't want him to get jittery and tire himself out before the race even started.

At last it was time. Alison glanced over her shoulder and saw Maimun in the crowd. The genie lifted one arm

in salute, and Alison thought she even saw him wink
at her.

"It isn't every day you have someone cheering you on
that nobody else can see, is it?" she murmured to Shihab.

A second later, the starter dropped his flag. The
horses leaped forward eagerly. Alison felt a tremendous
surge of power as Shihab took off beneath her. Balancing
skillfully in the saddle, she gave the stallion his head and
let him find his own stride. She kept her hands firm on
the reins, ready to steady him if he needed it. But the
horse had been born and bred to race in the desert, and
his footing was swift and sure. Out of the corner of her
eye, Alison saw that the bay horse to her left had already
been left in the dust, along with most of the others. But
the dapple gray was only a neck behind.

"Go, Shihab!" Alison called, her voice almost lost in
the rhythm of his powerful strides. "You can do it!"

Shihab's strong legs pounded along steadily over the
hot sand. This was nothing at all like riding the camel.
Alison laughed out loud for the sheer joy of Shihab's
speed. The wind snatched the sound almost before it
emerged from her throat, and Alison laughed again.

They reached the outcropping in what felt like mere
seconds, though Alison knew it must have taken longer
than that. As Shihab swept around it, the gray mare

pulled a little closer. Now she was only a nose behind.

"Come on, boy," Alison yelled as Shihab rounded the rocks. The desert landscape slipped away rapidly beneath her horse's flying hooves.

The two horses stayed close together through the foothills. As she rode, Alison caught glimpses of the men positioned here and there to mark the course. Each of them raised a hand or shouted in salute of the two leaders, and Alison did her best to wave back as she swept by.

They left the foothills and headed for the finish line, Shihab's powerful strides eating up the yards faster than Alison could have imagined. The mare was running just as fast, and for a moment the two horses were neck and neck. Alison crouched low over Shihab's withers and signaled him for more speed.

"Okay, boy," she cried. "Let's win this race!"

Shihab responded with a tremendous burst of speed. It was too much for the gray mare. She dropped back to a nose behind, then a neck. Before long, Alison couldn't see the other horse at all when she looked back. And when Shihab swept over the finish line, he was half a dozen yards ahead.

"Ya-hoo!" Alison shouted breathlessly, pumping one fist in the air. "We did it! We won!" She pulled

Shihab to a halt.

The sultan stepped down from his dais and walked over to Alison as she dismounted and gave Shihab an excited hug. "Excellent riding, stranger," he called. "Today you bring your family and your kingdom great honor. What is your name, my son?"

Alison smiled, glad that the sultan didn't recognize her. "My name is Ahmad, Your Majesty," she said, trying to make her voice deeper and gruffer than usual. "You do me great honor with your praise." She bowed low before him, and the sultan moved on to the second-place finisher.

"Great job, boy," Alison said, giving her horse another hug. "You're the best horse ever."

Suddenly Maimun appeared in a flash of silver light. "Not quite. But he is the fastest in the land."

"Maimun!" Alison cried. She was so excited by her victory that she impulsively reached out to hug him. Even though he looked rather airy and insubstantial, he felt solid and real as he hugged her back.

"Master," he said in a voice filled with wonder. "What are you doing?"

Alison stepped back and shrugged. "I'm glad you didn't leave without saying good-bye." She realized that she would miss him—and not just because of the wishes.

"Thanks for sticking around long enough to cheer me on."
She broke into a proud grin. "Did you see that ride? I
can't believe we won!"

Maimun looked slightly surprised. "Naturally you
won," he said. "You asked for the fastest horse, did you
not? How could it be otherwise?"

"Oh." Alison had to think about that one for a
moment. "So you mean my riding didn't have anything
to do with it?"

"Of course not," Maimun said. "Your wish mentioned
nothing of that."

Alison frowned. "But that means it wasn't a real race
at all," she said. "The others didn't even have a chance
of winning."

"That is correct," the genie replied.

Alison was speechless. Knowing that the race had
been decided before it even started took most of the
triumph out of it. Winning was great, but if you knew you
hadn't earned it yourself . . .

Finally she sighed. Real challenge or not, the desert
race had still been awfully exciting. She was glad she had
used her third wish to ride in it.

Maimun interrupted her thoughts. "I must bid you
farewell, Princess. It is time for me to depart."

"Good-bye, Maimun," Alison said, reaching out for

another hug. "It's been fun knowing you."

The genie's serious expression changed to one Alison had never seen on his face before—a smile. "Thank you, master," Maimun said. "You, too, have been most memorable. In fact, the next time a master asks the number of my previous masters, I shall be able to answer, 'More than one.'" He held up one slender finger.

Alison laughed. "Good-bye, Maimun."

"Good-bye, Princess," the genie replied. A second later, he was gone.

Alison smiled once more at the spot where he had been. She would remember Maimun—not as a mere genie, but as a friend.

The other riders began walking their mounts back toward the stable, and Alison fell in step with them, leading Shihab. When they arrived at the palace she handed his lead line to a groom, pausing for one last fond pat on the horse's shining chestnut neck. "Thanks for the ride, Shihab," she whispered in his alert, pointed ear. The horse snorted in response.

Minutes later Alison was in the palace bedchamber changing back into the rose-pink outfit. Fortunately, Fatima was nowhere to be seen. Alison picked up a gleaming silver tray, so shiny she could see her reflection in it clearly.

"Good-bye, Arabia," Alison murmured, taking one last look around. Then she lifted the tray and gazed at her own reflection until it began to shimmer and change.

Chapter
Eight

BROTHERLY
LOVE

lison looked around at the familiar sights of Ellie's
attic. She was home—almost. It didn't take her
long to change back into her regular clothes and put
everything back in the trunk. Then she ran downstairs,
pausing only to lock the attic door carefully behind her.

As she dropped the key back into its silver box, Ellie
stepped out of the sitting room. "Did you have a nice
time in the attic, Alison?"

"Definitely," Alison said. "I'll tell you about it another

time. Right now, there's something I have to do at home."

Ellie smiled. "Run along, then."

Moments later, Alison burst through the kitchen door and found her father cooking dinner while the twins jumped around him, getting in the way. Mark was sitting at the table cleaning mud off his baseball shoes.

"Hi, everyone," she said cheerfully.

Her father glanced at her. "Hi, sweetheart," he said. "Did you find your friends?"

"Not exactly," Alison replied. Before her father could ask any more questions, she grabbed the twins' hands in her own. "Come on, you two," she said. "How would you like to be grown-ups and help me make a salad?"

Her father smiled gratefully as Alison set the little boys to work washing lettuce. "Thanks, honey," he said. "They've been running me ragged. I don't know how you coped by yourself all day."

"It wasn't easy," Alison said with a rueful laugh. She wanted to apologize for being so grumpy earlier, but that could wait. Right now, she knew, the best thing she could do for her father was to help out.

Mark glanced up as she put a bottle of salad dressing on the table. "Why are you so helpful all of a sudden?" he asked.

Alison tossed her head. "I like being helpful," she replied. Seeing Mark's expression, she smiled. She didn't blame him for being surprised. She hadn't acted very happy to help earlier that day. But now she was happy to pitch in and do her part. "Besides, in case you didn't notice, food doesn't just appear on the table by magic." That reminded her of the dates she had accidentally wished for, and she giggled.

Mark looked suspicious. "What's so funny?"

Alison started to say, "your face," in response, but she stopped herself. Somehow, she just didn't feel like being mean to Mark right now. The Arabian palace had been a fascinating place, but it had been a lonely one, too. Except for Maimun, Alison hadn't really had anyone to talk to. The servants had just wanted to wait on her, and the sultan had been too busy. It was nice to be back with her family again. They might not be perfect—especially Mark—but they certainly made life more interesting. And they didn't need a single magic wish to do it.

Alison smiled at Mark. "Nothing's funny," she said. "I was just thinking about something."

Mark rolled his eyes. "There's a first time for everything," he said.

Alison laughed. It was good to be home.

Later that evening the living room phone rang. It was Keisha. Megan and Heather had eaten dinner at the Vances' house after skating, and they were listening on an extension.

"I'm glad you called!" Alison exclaimed. "I've been bursting to tell you about what happened to me today."

Alison told them all about her adventure. "It sounds like you had so much fun," Keisha said when she was finished.

Heather sighed dreamily. "Imagine getting to ride a horse, a camel, and a flying carpet, all in one adventure. I wish I'd been there."

"I wish you were, too," Alison said, resting the phone on her shoulder. "Maybe you could have helped me plan my wishes better so I wouldn't keep using them up by accident." She laughed. "Also, you could have helped me dodge the servants."

"Dodge them?" Keisha said. "Are you kidding? I wish I had a few servants around my house to help out with the chores. Don't you?"

"Well, maybe," Alison admitted. "But only if my family was still there, too. Servants just can't replace having them around."

Megan was surprised. "Really?" she said. "You mean if you found a genie in the garage next week, you wouldn't wish to trade in your brothers for your very own maid?"

Alison was silent for a moment. "I'll admit, it's a tempting thought. But that's one wish I hope never comes true." Just then she heard the front door open. "I'd better go, guys," Alison said. "I think my mom just got home. I'll see you tomorrow."

In the kitchen, Mrs. McCann set a bag of groceries on the counter. "Hi, pumpkin," she said. "I got the things we need for your bake sale."

Alison smiled. "Thanks, Mom."

"One of the recipes I made tonight gave me a great idea for an ingredient that will make your cookies extra moist." Mrs. McCann dug into the bag. "Ah, here we go," she said, pulling out a box. She held it up. "Dates."

Mrs. McCann looked very confused when Alison started to laugh.

Diary

Dear Diary,

I just had to write and say how much better I feel now that I've talked to Dad. Tonight I apologized to him for the way I acted earlier. And when I told him why I was so grumpy, because I sometimes feel like he and Mom like Mark better than me, he was pretty surprised. He didn't know I felt that way, and he told me it just isn't true. For one thing he reminded me of all the special stuff he and I do together. And he said that when Mark gets to do things first, it's just because he's older. I'll have my chance—Dad and Mom will make sure of it.

Well, we have a lot of baking to do tomorrow, so I guess I'd better get to sleep. I can't wait to help make Mom's special chocolate date cookies just as long as I don't have to eat any!

Love, Me

Alison